WITHDRAWN

FURRY AND FLO

capstone
young readers

Furry and Flo is published by
Capstone Young Readers
A Capstone Imprint
1710 Roe Crest Drive
North Mankato, MN 56003
www.capstoneyoungreaders.com

Text and Illustrations © 2014 Stone Arch Books

Library of Congress Cataloging-in-Publication Data
Troupe, Thomas Kingsley.
The problems with goblins / by Thomas Kingsley Troupe ; Illustrated by Stephen Gilpin.

    p. cm. -- (Furry and Flo)

Summary: Ten-year-old Flo has lived at Corman Towers for a week now, and while she
knows the apartment building is weird, she likes her new friend Furry--but three
goblins are trying to drag him to the other world, and Flo learns that even werewolves
can have secrets.

  ISBN 978-1-4342-5042-1 (library binding) -- ISBN 978-1-4342-6424-4 (ebook) --
ISBN 978-1-62370-034-8 (paper over board)

1. Werewolves--Juvenile fiction. 2. Goblins--Juvenile fiction. 3. Best friends--Juvenile
fiction. [1. Werewolves--Fiction. 2. Goblins--Fiction. 3. Secrets--Fiction. 4. Best friends-
-Fiction. 5. Friendship--Fiction.] I. Gilpin, Stephen., ill. II. Title.

PZ7.T7538Pro 2013

813.6--dc23

                                    2013002775

Artistic effects: Shutterstock/Kataleks Studio (background)

Book design by Hilary Wacholz

Printed in China by Nordica.
0413/CA21300444
032013   007226NORDF13

THE PROBLEMS WITH GOBLINS

BOOK 2

BY THOMAS KINGSLEY TROUPE
ILLUSTRATED BY STEPHEN GILPIN

TABLE OF

CONTENTS

PROLOGUE

Flo Gardner was pretty sure she'd seen it all. Even though she was only ten years old, she'd lived in more places than she could count. But Corman Towers was by far the strangest place she'd ever lived. Ever since she and her mom had moved into the giant apartment building in the middle of the city the week before, things had been weird.

On her first day there, she'd met Furry.

Furry was a weird name for a boy, but it fit. That's because Furry was a werewolf. He'd made Flo promise that she wouldn't tell anyone. Not even her mom.

And if having a werewolf for a neighbor wasn't weird enough, Flo had discovered a crack in the floor of the building's basement laundry room. It wasn't a normal crack — it was a sealed portal to another world. Except it wasn't so sealed up anymore. On her first night in Corman Towers, Flo had discovered that a giant spider had somehow managed to get through the crack. And the spider had laid eggs all over the apartment building.

Together, Furry and Flo had managed to get all the spider eggs — and more importantly, the giant spider mama — back through the crack to their own world. Then they'd sealed the crack up with an old bedspread. Case closed. Hopefully.

Yes, after a week in her new home, Flo had seen it all. Or so she thought.

PARK
BEFORE
DARK

CHAPTER 1

Flo sat on a swing in the playground in the park across from Corman Towers. Furry climbed to the top of the swing set and hung upside down by his legs.

"Flo, look," Furry cried. His T-shirt flipped down and covered his face. He laughed like it was the funniest thing in the whole world.

"You're going to get hurt," Flo warned him.

"Nah," Furry said. "Watch." He swung his body forward and did a flip in the air. Flo

gasped as he landed perfectly on his feet.
Furry raised his arms like a gymnast.

"Nice," Flo said. "But I thought only cats landed on their feet. Not werewolves."

Furry scanned the mostly empty playground to see if anyone else had seen his gymnastics. No else seemed to have noticed.

"If you don't want people to know you're not a normal kid, you might want to knock off the flips," Flo said. "Someone might see."

Furry walked over and hopped up into the swing next to Flo's. They swung together quietly for a while. Flo let her bare toes graze the top of her Dyno-Katz lunchbox, which lay in the sand, lid up.

It's getting pretty beat up, Flo thought as she stared at her beloved lunchbox. The picture of Kutty Kat was scuffed, and Acro Kat had a small dent near her face.

The lunchbox was a reminder of a different time. A better one.

Furry twisted back and forth in his swing, making the chains rattle noisily. On the other side of the park, a man threw a tennis ball for his big golden retriever. The ball bounced once before the dog snatched it out of the air. He turned and ran back to his owner, wagging his tail in excitement as he dropped the ball.

"Do you like playing fetch?" Flo asked, nodding at the man and his dog.

"Oh, very funny," Furry said. He rolled his eyes and laughed.

Across the park, the man threw the ball far and high. His dog took off after it, tearing across the open grass.

"I was just kid —" Flo started to say.

"Hold on," Furry interrupted. He suddenly jumped off of his swing and sprinted toward the soaring tennis ball.

"That ball isn't for you!" Flo yelled.

But Furry didn't even pause. Flo watched as the ball hit the ground and bounced toward the busy street.

"Oh, no," Flo whispered. The dog didn't seem to notice that the ball was headed straight into traffic. Neither did Furry, who was running after the dog as fast as he could. His feet barely seemed to touch the grass.

"Rocky!" the dog's owner yelled from the middle of the park. He took off after the dog, but Flo knew he'd never get there in time.

Furry was just a few steps behind Rocky. The dog bounded across the sidewalk and right into the busy street. Flo couldn't look away. She started running too.

Suddenly Furry dove forward and grabbed Rocky around his middle. A car slammed on its brakes, tires squealing and horn blaring.

At the last possible second, Furry leapt straight up into the air, carrying the golden retriever with him. He landed on the hood

of the car with the dog in his arms, safe and sound.

Flo stopped running and breathed a sigh of relief. On the hood of the car, the golden retriever licked Furry's face.

"Aw, knock it off," Furry said. He grinned and hopped off the car's hood. A moment later, Rocky's owner arrived.

"Wow," the guy said. "Thanks, kid."

"Sure thing," Furry said, setting Rocky down. "He would've done the same for me."

"That was incredible," Flo said, walking up. "And incredibly dumb, too."

"I don't know," Furry said with a shrug. He looked over at the man and his dog. The golden retriever was happily licking his owner's face. "If you can do something good, I think you should do it."

CHAPTER 2

After the dog and his owner had both walked off and the car had driven away, Flo remembered her lunchbox. She ran back over to the swings.

"Oh, thank goodness!" she said, scooping up her Dyno-Katz lunchbox and holding it close. She dusted sand from its sides. "I don't know what I would have done if it was gone."

Furry scratched behind his ear and raised

an eyebrow. "What's up with that lunchbox?" he asked.

"Have you ever seen one like it?" Flo asked.

"No," Furry replied. "I guess not."

"That's because I have the only one in the whole entire world," Flo said. "If I lost it I could never replace it."

"You could get a different one," Furry said. "Lots of people have lunchboxes. They just don't bring them everywhere like you do."

"That's because no one else has a Dyno-Katz lunchbox," Flo said. "Just me. It's special."

Furry shook his head. "What's so special about it?" he asked. "I've never even heard of the Dyno-Katz."

"My dad gave it to me," Flo whispered. She swallowed hard. "Anyway, we should get back. Do you still want to eat at my place?"

"Yeah, okay," Furry replied. "I'm pretty hungry."

Flo laughed. "You're always hungry," she said. "Let's go."

* * *

Flo's mom set two bowls of bright yellow macaroni and cheese in front of them. Flo picked up her spoon and shoveled a mouthful of noodles into her mouth. But Furry made no move to touch his.

"I thought you said you were hungry," Flo said.

"Yeah," Furry said. "I am."

Flo watched in horror as Furry

proceeded to scoop out a pile of macaroni and cheese with his bare hand. He left the spoon right where it was next to the bowl.

"What're you doing?" Flo asked, looking at him in shock. "Quit acting like an animal and use a spoon!"

Furry ignored her, instead continuing to eat straight out of his hand. "Uh canth uth dat," he said, his mouth full.

"What?" Flo said. "I can't understand a word you're saying."

Furry waited until he swallowed. Then he pointed at the shiny spoon sitting next to his bowl with a cheese-covered finger. "That," he said. "I can't use that spoon."

Flo sighed impatiently. "Okay," she said. "What's wrong with the spoon?"

Furry glanced over at Flo's mom, who was

busy pulling the garbage bag out of the plastic can. She didn't appear to be listening, but Furry seemed cautious anyway.

"It's silver," he whispered.

"Yeah," Flo said. "Our regular silverware isn't unpacked yet, so my mom pulled out the fancy stuff. So what?"

Furry rolled his eyes. "So I'm sort of allergic to silver," he muttered under his breath. "Get it?" He glanced nervously at Flo's mom again to make sure she wasn't listening.

Flo looked at him like he'd grown a second head.

"You don't know much about werewolves, do you," Furry said. "Silver bullets? Silver chains? Silver anything? Not good for me."

"Oh," Flo replied in a hushed voice. "Is that stuff really true?"

Furry just stared back at her, eyebrows raised. "Well I'm not using the spoon, am I?" he said pointedly.

"Got it," Flo replied. "Sorry."

Furry scooped up another handful and stuffed it into his mouth. Noodles and cheese sauce dribbled down his chin.

"I have to run this down to the Dumpster," Flo's mom called. "I'll be right back." She twisted the garbage bag closed and walked out of the room without a glance at the mess Furry had made.

"I'm going to get sick watching you eat," Flo said. She hopped up from her seat and walked into the small kitchen. "You're not allergic to plastic, are you?"

"No," Furry mumbled with his mouth full of pasta.

Flo found a plastic spoon and set it down next to Furry's bowl. She snatched up the silver spoon and tossed it into the sink, far away from Furry.

"Thanks," Furry said.

Flo sat back down. "So, I have a million questions," she said and stirred the macaroni around her bowl. "About werewolf stuff."

"Okay," Furry responded.

Flo watched the door to make sure her mom didn't walk back in and overhear them. "So how do you —" she started to say.

"I found him!" a strange voice suddenly interrupted. "I found him!"

Furry and Flo turned and saw a small, green creature staring back at them. His yellow eyes widened when he realized that he'd been spotted.

"Uh-oh," the creature cried.

Before Flo could breathe, the little creature ran away.

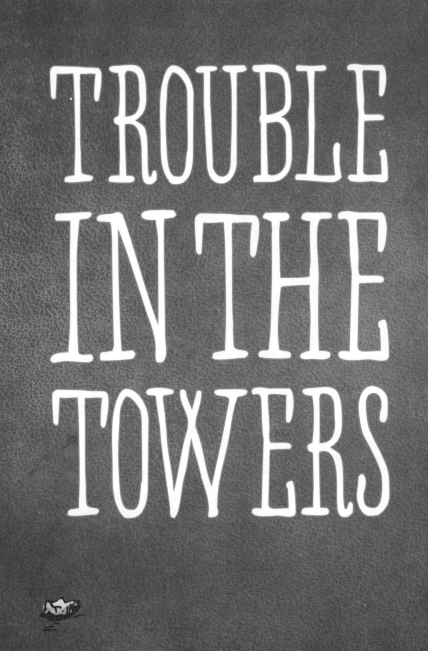

TROUBLE IN THE TOWERS

CHAPTER 3

Furry jumped up and ran full speed after the little creature. It had disappeared down the narrow hallway that led to Flo's bedroom. Flo followed quickly behind, her spoon still in her hand.

"What was that thing?" she called, charging down the hallway after Furry. She saw a dirty foot disappear through her bedroom door.

"A goblin!" Furry shouted as he leapt into her room. He bounced on Flo's bed and fell into the space between the mattress and wall with a loud *crash!*

Across the room, Flo saw the goblin's backside disappearing through her open window. The creature kicked his feet and grunted as he squeezed his way outside. He landed on the fire escape with a *thud!*

"A goblin?" Flo repeated. Her mouth dropped open in shock. *A werewolf is weird enough*, she thought. *Now I have to deal with goblins, too?*

Furry stood up and opened the window wider. He poked his head outside. "He went downstairs!" he cried, turning to Flo.

"Good," Flo said. "Let him go! Don't we want the creepy goblin to stay outside? I sure don't want him in here!"

Furry shook his head. "You don't understand," he said, looking serious. "The problem with goblins is there's never just one. They travel in packs. And they cause all sorts of trouble."

Just then, Flo heard her mom come back into the apartment. The door slammed closed behind her.

"Close the window," Flo hissed frantically. "I don't want my mom to think we're doing something dumb like climbing out onto the fire escape. No more crazy stunts, remember?"

"Kids?" Mom called. "You need to finish eating!"

"We'll be right there," Flo called back. "I was just . . . um . . . showing Furry where the bathroom is."

Furry ran down the hall to the bathroom. He flushed the toilet once and ran the water in the sink like he was washing his hands.

"Yeah, you'd better make sure he doesn't get lost," Mom replied with a laugh. "In our HUGE apartment!"

Flo laughed too. Their apartment was beyond tiny. But at least they could laugh about it.

If Mom's happy, I can try to be happy too, Flo thought.

Just then, Furry rejoined her in the hallway. "So what're we going to do about the goblins?" he whispered as they headed back to the kitchen. "They're serious trouble."

"So you really think there's more than one?" Flo asked.

"I don't *think* so," Furry said pointedly. "I know so."

* * *

It was hard to sit down and finish eating with goblins on the loose, but Flo's mom wouldn't let them leave until they were done. When they finished, they headed out into the hallway. Flo gripped her lunchbox tightly.

"It's the crack again, isn't it?" Flo asked. "Did those goblins come out of there?"

"Who knows?" Furry replied, avoiding Flo's gaze.

"But I thought we plugged that thing up!" Flo cried.

"For now," Furry said. "But Curtis has tried to keep it closed for years. It doesn't seem to stop crazy stuff from coming out of there."

"Fantastic," Flo said. She remembered Curtis, Corman Towers' old, retired maintenance man, warning them about the cracked seal. A moment later, she remembered something else.

"Wait a second," Flo said. She narrowed her eyes at Furry. "Why did that goblin say 'I found him'? He pointed right at you when he said it."

Furry looked back at his apartment door. "It's ... um ... kind of a long story," he said. "We don't have time!"

And he was right. A door down the hall burst open, and two more goblins came charging down the hallway, one riding on the other's shoulders. A TV was blaring at top volume inside the apartment they'd just exited.

Suddenly the goblin on the bottom tripped. They both went flying, landing on their large noses and pinched green faces. A remote control fell out of one goblin's hand and clattered to the floor. The goblins quickly clambered to their feet and ran down the hallway, away from Furry and Flo.

Furry and Flo exchanged a look and took off down the hall after the creatures. At the end of the hallway, the goblins jumped up to reach the garbage chute. Without a word, they pushed open the flap and threw themselves down the chute.

"Those guys are nuts," Furry muttered. He and Flo stopped in the middle of the hallway. Flo bent down to pick up the discarded remote. The noise coming from inside the apartment was still deafening.

Just then, a large man in a Hawaiian shirt appeared in the apartment's open doorway. "You!" he shouted at Flo. "You took my remote? How did you get in here?"

"Me?" Flo exclaimed. She shook her head. "No! It was the —"

"I'm sorry, Dr. Fuller," Furry interrupted. He grabbed the remote from Flo's hand and turned the TV volume down before handing it to Dr. Fuller. "My friend is new here. She forgot which apartment was hers. It was an honest mistake."

Dr. Fuller's face had turned as red as a cherry Popsicle. "Just make sure you have the right apartment next time," he grumbled.

"Yes, sir" Flo said, and nodded. "I sure will."

Dr. Fuller just stared at the two of them. He seemed to be waiting for something.

"Uh . . . I'm sorry I took your remote?" Flo said. She didn't know what else he expected her to say.

"You two seem like you're up to no good," Dr. Fuller said, looking back and forth between Furry and Flo. "You'd better watch it. I don't like trouble."

"Believe us, we don't like it either," Furry said. "Not at all."

CHAPTER 4

Once Dr. Fuller finished lecturing them and closed the door to his apartment, Furry headed toward the garbage chute.

"Where are you going?" Flo called, running after him.

"To get rid of those goblins," Furry said. "They'll never leave me . . . uh, I mean us . . . alone if I don't get rid of them."

He pushed open the flap to the garbage chute. He peered into the hole and whistled.

"You're not jumping in there, are you?" Flo asked. "We're seventeen floors up."

"Nah," Furry said. He let the door swing closed. "It's tempting, but I know where the garbage room is."

"Oh, yay," Flo muttered sarcastically. "The trash room. Just the place I've always dreamed of visiting. How soon can we get there?"

Furry grinned at her, completely missing her sarcasm. "Cool! I'm glad you're excited. I was afraid I'd have to take care of these guys myself."

"I'm not ex —" Flo started to say. She sighed. "Oh, never mind. Forget it. Let's just get this over with."

Furry and Flo headed back to the elevator and pushed the down button. "Too bad it's not a full moon," Flo said. She watched as the numbered buttons lit up, marking their descent to the basement. "You could turn into a werewolf and just eat those guys. Problem solved."

Furry grinned at her mischievously. Then he pinched his nose shut and held his breath. Fur sprouted from his skin, and his back and face stretched out until he had transformed into a canine version of himself. He had become a werewolf.

Even though Flo had seen Furry change once before, it still took her by surprise. She stumbled back in fear and crammed herself into the corner of the elevator. Her lunchbox dropped from her hand.

"Ta-da!" Furry said. "But there's still one problem: I don't eat meat."

"Seriously?" Flo said. She crouched down to scoop up her Dyno-Katz lunch box. "A vegetarian werewolf?"

"Yeah," Furry said. He sniffed the elevator car. "I've never really had a taste for it. That could change at any time, though." He smiled at Flo with his long, sharp teeth.

"Knock it off," Flo said and pushed him away. She knew Furry was only kidding, but still. It was creepy.

"I'm just messing around," Furry said. "Sheesh."

"How did you do that?" Flo asked. "Change, I mean. I thought werewolves only changed on a full moon."

"Well, yeah," Furry said. "On a full moon, I change no matter what. But I can change when I want, too. Do your ears ever get plugged up? Or pop when you're driving up a big hill?"

"Sure," Flo said, sounding a bit confused. "Why?"

"So, you know how you can plug your nose, close your mouth, and sort of blow to unplug them?" Furry explained. "Well, when I do it, I change."

Furry looked up at the numbers above the elevator's double doors. They were getting close to the basement. "I have to change back. Got anything to drink in there?" he asked, motioning to Flo's Dyno-Katz lunchbox.

Flo opened the lid and handed over the juice box she kept inside. Furry snatched it up, tore the top off, and drained the entire thing in one gulp.

"You'd better hurry up. We're almost

there," Flo said as they passed the second floor.

"Quit worrying so much," Furry told her. He let out a loud burp, and the gray fur covering his body immediately disappeared. His paws shrunk back to regular human hands, and his long, canine face returned to its normal shape.

Furry the werewolf was replaced by a boy in a pair of torn shorts just as the basement button lit up on the elevator and the doors slid open.

"Aw, man. I ripped my pants," Furry said, looking down at his clothes. "My mom is *not* going to be happy."

Flo stared at her strange new friend in amazement. "So, you burp to become normal again?" she said. For a moment, she forgot that they were supposed to be hunting troublesome goblins.

"Well, yeah," Furry said. He wiped the juice mustache from his upper lip. "If you can call humans normal, that is. I mean, personally, I think werewolves are pretty normal."

"I really don't know anything about werewolves," Flo whispered. She took a cautious step out into the dark hallway. "Or goblins."

Furry followed close behind her as the elevator doors slid closed behind them, trapping them in the basement. "You will."

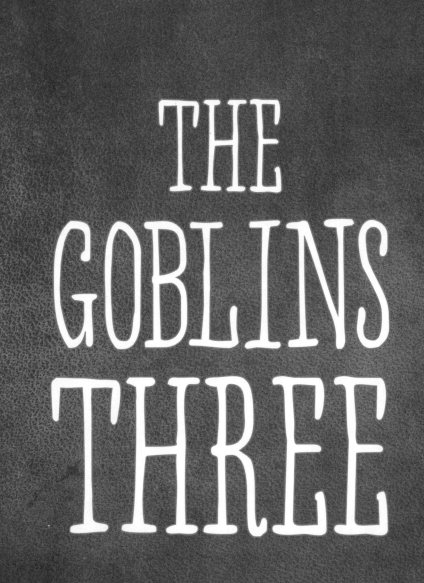

THE
GOBLINS
THREE

CHAPTER 5

Flo and Furry hurried down the basement hallway, past the laundry room, and around a corner. Flo could tell they were close to the garbage and recycling room because the stench kept getting stronger. It smelled like wet cardboard, dirty diapers, and oddly enough, tacos.

"Oh, man," Flo said, plugging her nose. "That's ripe."

"Try having my sense of smell," Furry said. He looked sick to his stomach. "It feels like my nose is on fire."

Voices and the sound of clanking glass came from an open doorway. Furry and Flo peeked around the corner and into the room. On top of the overflowing trash bags sat the nasty goblins from upstairs.

"He's upstairs," the goblin from Flo's apartment cried. "I smelled that it was he!"

The largest goblin threw a bag of garbage against the wall. It tore open and dumped coffee grounds, orange peels, and food wrappers everywhere. "Quiet, Dungton," the big goblin snapped. "The Goblins Three all have to agree."

"Yes, yes," the smallest goblin squawked. "Snottle speaks wise." He tossed an empty pickle jar on the ground, flinging shattered glass everywhere.

"But I saw him, Wartis!" Dungton cried. He brushed Styrofoam packing peanuts off the sleeve of his bare arm and clenched his hand into a small fist. "I know he is the one. He fears silver!"

Flo pulled her head back into the hallway and looked at Furry, wide-eyed. "They *are* after you," she whispered. "Why? What do they want with you?"

"I'm not sure," Furry said quietly. "But we have to do something."

"Why don't we tell them to scram," Flo suggested.

"Are you crazy? You can't just tell goblins to . . ." Furry began, but he was too late. Flo had already walked into the garbage room.

The three goblins all fell silent as Flo stepped into the room. Dungton raised an eyebrow above one of his bulging yellow eyes.

"Hey, goblins," Flo called. She stood in the doorway with her hands planted firmly on her hips and glared at them. Her lunchbox dangled from her left hand. "Why don't you get lost?"

Dungton leapt up from the pile of trash he'd been perched on and immediately landed face first on a waterlogged loaf of bread. He stood up and chunks of wet bread fell off of his long, pointy nose.

"She was with him!" the goblin hollered, pointing at Flo. "This girl befriended the wolf boy!"

Flo glared back at Dungton. "You shouldn't point at people," she told him. "It's *rude.*"

"Tell us where the boy is, girlie," Dungton
snapped back.

"Why should I?" Flo asked. She watched as
the biggest goblin, Snottle, climbed down from
his garbage pile with a grunt and a wheeze.
The goblin leader took a bite from a half-
eaten hot dog and tossed the rest over his
shoulder.

"We are the Goblins Three," Snottle said in a rough, gravely voice. "We've come to fetch the one who flees."

"What?" Flo said. "Furry doesn't have fleas!"

Snottle glared at her. "Hand over the wolf boy, and we'll trouble you no longer."

Flo stared at the three disgusting-looking goblins. They stared back at her with their awful yellow eyes, waiting for her to tell them where Furry was. The faint buzz of the fluorescent lights was the only sound in the smelly room.

"I don't know any wolf boy," Flo lied. "You must have the wrong apartment building."

"She lies!" Dungton shouted. He pointed at her again. Drool dripped from his jagged teeth. "I can smell him!"

"Stop pointing at me!" Flo shouted. "Do it again, and I'll knock your lights out!" She held up her Dyno-Katz lunchbox like a weapon to show she meant business.

"Point, point, point!" Dungton snarled. He pointed at her each time he said it.

"That's it," Flo cried, swinging her lunchbox at the goblin. "I warned you! Lights out!"

Flo swung her lunchbox back behind her shoulder, clipping the light switch on the wall behind her in the process. As promised, the lights went out.

"Run, Furry!" Flo shouted. She dashed out of the trash room and back into the hallway. In the dim light, she could see Furry was already several steps ahead of her. She hurried after him, her lunchbox banging against her leg as she ran.

"Get them!" Snottle shouted furiously from inside the dark room. "Get them both!"

"Ow!" one of the other goblins cried. "You stepped on my foot!"

"Hold on to that dumb lunchbox," Furry growled back at Flo. "You're going to lead them right to us if you keep making noise!"

"My lunchbox isn't dumb," Flo snapped. "It saved me in there. Besides, your yelling isn't helping!"

Flo cradled the lunchbox closer to her chest. She could hear the contents slide around with every step. She followed Furry past Curtis's apartment, around a corner, and through an open doorway into another crowded room.

At least this one smells better than the trash room, Flo thought.

It was so dark that Flo was afraid she'd run straight into a wall. Instead, she ran straight into Furry. She caught a glimpse of her friend's face, expecting him to be mad.

But Furry wasn't angry. He was terrified.

"Where are we?" Flo asked. "Can we turn a light on?"

"Not unless we want those goblins to find us," Furry said. "We need some time to come up with a plan to get rid of them."

"What is this place?" Flo asked, looking around the dark, crowded room.

"It's the storage room," Furry said. "There are a bunch of lockers in here. People keep their bikes and other stuff down here. Stuff that takes up too much room in an apartment. I hide here sometimes during the full moon until I change back."

"You just wait it out in here?" Flo asked. It was too dark to see much, but it seemed very dark and lonely.

"Yep," Furry said. He reached out and took Flo's hand. "I'll show you where I hide."

Farther down the hall, the Goblins Three scrambled across the tiled floor. Garbage clattered as they got closer.

"Okay," Flo said, following Furry into the darkness.

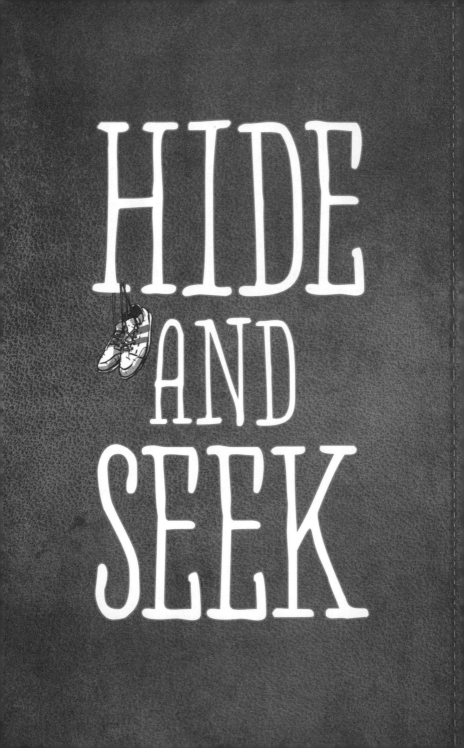

CHAPTER 6

"How can you see where we're going?" Flo whispered as she and Furry slipped between two wooden beams. She couldn't tell where she was, but it felt like a maze of shelves and aisles. Her shoulder brushed up against what felt like a padlock.

"Wolves have good vision," Furry said.

"Even when you're, you know, just Furry?" Flo asked.

"I'm always Furry," he said. "But yeah. Even when I'm a human, I can see and smell things better. It's best when I'm a werewolf."

"Cool," Flo whispered.

"Here we are," Furry said. He crouched down and pulled Flo down beside him. "It's not very big, but we can wait here while we figure out a better plan."

Flo sat down. She could barely see the floor in the faint light from the hallway, but it felt cold and dirty. Both she and Furry listened quietly for a few minutes.

"I don't hear them," Flo whispered.

"That's not good," Furry said. "They're probably upstairs tearing up another apartment trying to find me."

Flo sort of hoped that was true. Maybe then someone else would take care of

the problem. But then she remembered
something her dad used to tell her. *Don't wait
for someone else to do what you're supposed
to, Flo. When it's up to you, it's up to you.*

"So why are they after you?" Flo asked.
"They said something about being after the
one who flees. Or maybe it was the one *with*
fleas . . . I can't remember."

Furry looked startled. "Well, I don't have
fleas," he said quickly. He paused, then added,
"I did once, but not anymore."

Flo shifted on the floor, trying to get
comfortable. She got the feeling Furry was
keeping something from her, but she didn't
know what. And it was getting on her nerves.

"So why, then?" Flo asked. "What's up with
these three goblin guys?"

"I don't really know," Furry whispered.

Just then, there was a scraping sound nearby. For an instant, the small amount of light coming from the hallway was blocked out.

"Someone is in here," Furry whispered.

"The goblins?" Flo gripped the handle of her lunchbox, ready to clobber anyone who got close. "Can you smell them?"

"No," Furry said, but he still sounded scared. "I think —"

"What are you two doing down there?" a voice boomed. A moment later, a flash of light blinded them.

WHAT DID YOU DO?

CHAPTER 7

"Curtis," Furry whispered loudly. "Turn the light off! They're going to find us!"

Curtis clicked the flashlight off. A moment later, a small, bare bulb above them lit up the room.

"What have you two done?" Curtis asked. He wore a pair of green fleece pajama pants and a thin yellow T-shirt with a picture of a superhero on the front. Curtis's eyes looked enormous behind the thick, round glasses he always wore.

"We didn't do anything," Furry replied. He stood up and brushed off his torn shorts. "There are three goblins chasing us! We think they came through the crack in the laundry room."

"I told you two to stay away from that blasted crack," Curtis snapped. "Who knows what will come out if you mess with it!"

"We're not messing with it! We tried to close it up," Flo said, climbing to her feet, too. "We stuffed a blanket in there. I haven't been there since."

Curtis looked at Flo, then back at Furry, who didn't say anything.

"Maybe *you* haven't," Curtis said. "But what about him?" He pointed right at Furry.

"I . . . um . . . I might've taken a peek," Furry said, avoiding their gazes. "Just a quick one, though!"

"Furry!" Flo said. "You opened the seal again? You let those goblins in here?"

"No," Furry insisted, shaking his head back and forth. "I closed it back up, just like we left it. Everything was fine when I left it."

"Well, clearly everything isn't fine now," Flo said.

"Okay," Furry said. "I know what to do. No more messing around."

Curtis stepped off to the side. "Did you see the mess they left everywhere?" he asked. "You two are responsible for the mess they've made. I don't clean or fix stuff up anymore. I'm retired!"

"I know," Furry said quietly. "Let's go, Flo."

He grabbed her by the hand, and together they headed for the elevator.

* * *

When Furry and Flo walked into the lobby, it was complete chaos. Pieces of the fake plants used to spruce up the building's entrance were scattered across the floor. The rug that used to lie in front of the door had been rolled into a long, tube-like shape. The newspapers near the mailboxes had been torn apart.

As Flo watched, Wartis picked up the rolled-up rug and swung it like a baseball bat, knocking a chair across the room. Snottle stood at the panel of buzzers that connected the lobby to the various apartments. He pushed them all at once and hollered into the speaker whenever someone answered.

"Who's there?" a woman's voice asked through the speaker.

"Human!" Snottle roared back. "Send the wolf boy to me!"

"What?" the confused voice replied. "Who is this?"

The goblin ignored her and pressed the next button.

Dungton ran down the main hallway. He tried to open doors and kicked the metal fire extinguisher boxes that hung along the walls. Pieces of garbage fell from his pockets and shirt as he moved along.

They're going to tear this place apart if they don't find what they want, Flo thought. *Or* who *they want.*

Just then, Furry let go of her hand and stepped bravely forward. "Enough!" he yelled.

The three goblins stopped in their tracks and stared at Furry with their round, yellow eyes.

"It's him, it's him," Dungton yelled. He ran back toward the lobby, almost skipping with delight. His foot caught a bump in the carpet, and he fell to the floor, landing on his face again.

The goblin quickly clambered to his feet and pointed at Furry. "It's the wolf boy in human form!"

Flo glanced around, but there was no one else there to hear Furry's secret. She was amazed that none of the other tenants had come out of their apartments.

At least not yet.

"You need to leave," Furry said. "All three of you."

"Ah, but we cannot," Snottle said. "Not until we bring you back."

Furry's shoulders sagged. He turned and looked back at Flo, his mouth curled in defeat. "I don't want to go," he said.

"What do they mean, bring you back? Back

where?" Flo asked. She turned to face the goblins. "You're not taking Furry anywhere. Now get lost!"

"The Goblins Three cannot leave until we return with the one who flees," Snottle said, as if reciting a poem. "Run again, and we'll tear this tower to rubble."

As the goblin recited his strange poem, Flo realized she'd misunderstood him the first time. The goblin leader hadn't meant *fleas* like the bug.

He meant flees as in running away, Flo thought. *But where did Furry flee from?*

CHAPTER 8

"Come with us wolf boy, and we'll trouble you no longer," Snottle growled in his rough, raspy voice.

The goblin took a couple of menacing steps toward Furry as if to prove there was no escape. "You do not belong here," he continued.

At their leader's words, Wartis and Dungton both crept closer to Furry. They had their gnarled hands outstretched like they were getting ready to grab him.

Flo raised her lunchbox in the air menacingly. She wasn't sure what good it would do, but it was all she had. Apparently goblins didn't really believe in talking things out.

"I'm not coming with you," Furry said. He took a deep breath and puffed out his bare chest. "If you want me to come, you'll have to drag me back!"

With that, Furry pinched his nose closed between his thumb and pointer finger. His body stretched, and within seconds his skin had been replaced by thick fur. His ears changed until they were tall and pointy sitting atop his canine head. Flo heard his shorts rip again as he changed.

The goblins looked stunned at Furry's transformation. Wartis backed up as fast as his goblin feet would carry him and tripped over an upside-down plant in the process. Dungton cowered behind an overturned end table.

Only Snottle didn't seem intimidated. He stepped forward again. "Seize him!" the goblin leader yelled.

Dungton ran at Furry, his hands outstretched to grab the little werewolf. But Furry was too fast for him. He quickly darted to the side and grabbed the goblin's arm, throwing Dungton across the lobby toward the candy machine at the other end.

The goblin's head bounced off of the plastic window, and he fell onto his back with a wheeze.

"Don't make this any harder than it has to be, wolf boy," Wartis warned. He snuck up behind Furry and grabbed a clump of the werewolf's thick gray fur.

Flo immediately dashed forward and swung her lunchbox at the goblin's hand to free her friend. But her aim wasn't as good as she'd thought.

"Hey!" Furry yelped as the lunchbox hit him too. He spun around fiercely, but when he saw Flo had helped him, he smiled at her, baring a mouthful of sharp teeth. "I mean, thanks!"

"Ouch," Wartis whimpered, clutching his hand close to his chest protectively. "That wasn't very nice, girlie."

"Leave my friend alone," Flo boomed furiously. She raised her lunchbox again.

"Touch him again, and I'll bonk you on the head next time!"

Snottle ran forward, his eyes narrowed with anger. He shoved Wartis out of the way and dove for Furry. Before the werewolf could react, the goblin had tackled him and pinned him to the ground. Furry bared his teeth in an angry growl, but Snottle wasn't intimidated. He growled right back.

"Get off of me!" Furry roared. He thrashed around on the ground, trying to get free.

"Not a chance, wolf!" Snottle spat back. He grabbed one of Furry's arms and pinned it against the tile floor. Flo stepped forward and raised her lunchbox in the air again. But before she could bring it down on Snottle's head, a hand caught hers, stopping the attack mid-strike.

"That's enough from you, girlie," Dungton snapped, gripping Flo's arm tightly. His long fingernails dug into her wrist, and he smelled like the wet garbage that had seeped into his ratty clothes.

"Let me go!" Flo screeched. She tried to pull free, but the goblin held tightly. Wartis grabbed her other arm to stop her thrashing.

There was no escape.

"Aye," Snottle grumbled, his face close to Furry's. "We've caught your wee girlfriend now and —"

"I'm not his girlfriend!" Flo shouted.

"Surrender and she's free to go," Snottle said. When Furry shifted his weight again, Snottle pressed his knee into the werewolf's stomach to pin him down. "You're bested, wolf."

Flo desperately tried to shake off the two goblins that held her captive. She had to pull free and help Furry, but the two who had her refused to let go.

"I don't want to hurt you," Wartis said. "I really don't."

"Quiet, Wart," Dungton hollered. "Keep your grip on her!"

Furry whined like a dog that needed to be let outside. "This is my home now," Furry whispered so softly that Flo almost didn't hear him.

"This place was never your home," Snottle replied angrily. He didn't seem to have any pity for the trapped werewolf. "And your fight is done."

Flo felt so helpless she wanted to cry. She couldn't do anything to help her friend.

"This is his home!" Flo yelled, holding back the tears. "His parents will miss him if you take him away!"

"Aye. They do miss him, girl," Dungton said. The goblin readjusted his grip on her arm. "That's why they sent us here."

Flo felt like she'd been punched in the stomach. "What does he mean, Furry?" she asked, her voice shaky. "Someone better tell me the truth!"

Furry whined again and turned to look up at Flo. "I came out of the cracked seal in the basement, too," he said. "That's why the seal won't close. I escaped my world to live in this one, and I don't ever want to go back."

CHAPTER 9

Flo felt dizzy. She stood there, unable to speak.

"That's why I didn't want you to say anything about what I really am," Furry said quietly. "People can't know about me."

"I don't understand," Flo whispered. She had so many questions that she didn't even know where to begin. But she didn't have to worry — Snottle didn't give her a chance.

"Quiet!" Snottle snapped. "The both of you! The offer remains. Come without a fight, wolf, and we'll let your human friend go free. I'll speak the Goblin's Oath that no harm will come to her."

"Don't do it, Furry," Flo said. "There has to be another way! We can —"

But Furry didn't listen to her. "Okay," he said with a sigh. "I'll do it." His shoulders slumped to the ground like the fight had gone out of him. "I'll go back home if you let Flo go."

"No, Furry!" Flo cried, desperately trying to yank free again. "You can't go back! This is your home now!"

Furry shook his head as Snottle pulled him to his feet. "It's not worth you getting hurt over me, Flo," he said. "It's okay. I'll go. This is all my fault."

Flo stared at Furry, trying to figure out if he had a new plan hidden up his sleeve. But Furry didn't look like he had anything hidden. He just looked defeated.

This is it, Flo thought. *They're really going to take him away. Back to whatever world he really came from. And I'll never see him again.*

As the realization hit her, a tear finally managed to sneak out of Flo's eye before she could stop it.

"Smart choice, wolf boy," Snottle growled. He turned toward his goblin minions. "To the seal!"

* * *

The goblins dragged Furry and Flo down to the laundry room. Somehow they managed to get there without running into anyone else. The laundry room was empty when they arrived, but a dryer hummed in the corner, and clothes tumbled around inside.

I wonder when whoever it is will be back

for their laundry, Flo thought. *Probably not soon enough.*

The goblins dragged Furry and Flo behind the dryers where the glowing blue crack was hidden. When they'd first discovered it, Curtis had told them that the crack used to separate their world from one filled with monsters and other creepy creatures. But at some point, the seal had been broken. Now all sorts of monsters occasionally found their way from their world to Earth. And into Corman Towers.

Including Furry, apparently, Flo thought.

The goblins pushed Furry closer to the glowing blue line.

"Can I at least say goodbye to my friend?" Furry asked. He twisted to look at Snottle, who was still holding Furry's arms behind his back. "I'm never going to see her again."

"Fine, but make it quick," Snottle growled. "Once we pass back through, there is no coming back."

Flo tried to blink back her tears, but she did a lousy job of it. She couldn't help it. Her eyes filled and tears trickled down her cheeks.

"I'm sorry, Flo," Furry said. "I should have told you the truth. I was just scared."

"It's okay," Flo said. "Really. I understand why you didn't."

"I wish I could stay so we could be friends for longer than a week," Furry added.

"Me too," Flo said. She couldn't believe this was actually goodbye. Furry was the only good thing about Corman Towers. *It's not fair*, Flo thought.

"Right," Dungton said, still gripping Flo's arm tightly. "That's enough. Let's go."

Furry took a deep breath and nodded. "Okay," he said. "Bye, Flo." He glanced at the goblins. "Let's get this over with."

"Bye, Furry," Flo said, wiping her eyes.

The goblins let go of Flo's arms and moved toward the glowing blue crack. The second Flo was free, Furry wrenched his arms out of Snottle's grip. He lunged forward and knocked Wartis's feet out from under him. The smallest goblin fell to the ground, bounced on the dirty floor, and fell through the glowing seal. He disappeared with a sudden *whump!*

"Hey!" Dungton shouted in surprise. He turned and jabbed a long, jagged fingernail into Furry's wolf chest. "You said —"

"I said you shouldn't point at people," Flo told him. "It's rude!"

With that, Flo turned and swung her

lunchbox at the garbage-covered goblin as hard as she could. The blow caught the goblin in the shoulder, and he stumbled sideways toward the seal.

Dungton's foot grazed the edge of the crack and he tumbled into it. A moment later, he followed Wartis through the broken seal with a loud *fwooomp!*

"You're going in after them!" Snottle shouted, his face twisted in anger. He lunged toward Furry, ready to push the little werewolf into the gaping blue crack after the two goblins.

But Furry was too fast. He leaped out of the goblin's path at the last possible second, and Snottle went flying past him. The big goblin's foot sank into the blue crack, and he was pulled down into the mysterious seal. *Shoomph!*

Furry looked over at Flo and smiled. "That was too close for comfort," he said with a sigh of relief.

"No kid —" Flo started to say.

But before she could finish her sentence, a gnarled green hand reached back up through the crack in the floor. It latched onto Furry's

ankle and yanked him down into the blue
abyss.

In an instant, Furry was sucked though the
seal with a loud *whooosh!*

"No!" Flo screamed. She fell to her knees,
inches from the crack. Her lunchbox clattered
to the floor of the laundry room.

But there was nothing she could do. Furry
was gone.

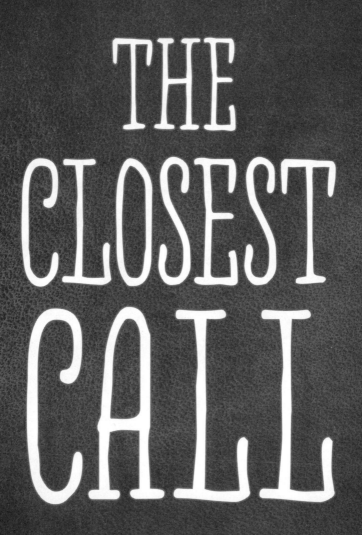

THE
CLOSEST
CALL

CHAPTER 10

Flo stared helplessly at the crack in the floor. Furry had done all he could to keep from going back to his world. And it hadn't been enough.

Now Flo was alone.

She thought about jumping into the crack after him, but remembered what Snottle had said. *"Once we pass back through, there is no coming back."*

She couldn't do it. As much as she wanted to go after Furry, Flo knew she couldn't just leave her mom behind. She needed Flo more than ever now that her dad was gone.

Besides, who knew what lurked on the other side of the cracked seal? If the giant spiders and mean, smelly goblins were a taste of Furry's world, Flo didn't want any part of it.

What am I going to do? Flo thought. *How am I supposed to explain to Furry's parents what happened to him? I have to tell them something. If they think Furry is lost or missing, they'll be worried sick.*

She thought about what Furry had said to her at the park after he rescued the dog. *If you can do something good, I think you should do it.*

Even though he had been keeping a pretty

huge secret from her, Furry was probably the best friend Flo had ever had. And he'd put her safety ahead of his own to protect her from the goblins. She couldn't just abandon him.

Flo heard the dryer buzz behind her, signaling it was finished. The drum inside the machine slowed down until it finally came to a stop.

Flo leaned over the glowing crack, careful not to touch it. "Furry?" she called into it. "Can you hear me?"

There was no response . . . at least not from Furry's world.

"Flo, is that you back there?" came Curtis's voice. "You'd better not be messing with that seal again. I warned you two to leave it alone. I don't need you two stirring up more trouble."

Flo poked her head up from behind the

bank of dryers to see Curtis shuffling across the room.

"Yeah, it's me," Flo said. She sniffed quietly. "I'm back here."

Curtis squeezed through the narrow space between the dryers and the wall. He joined Flo in the small area where the crack in the floor was hidden.

"You kids manage to get rid of the goblins?" he asked.

Flo nodded and felt tears trickle down her face again. She didn't want to cry in front of Curtis, but she didn't think she could stop it.

"We got rid of Furry, too," she said, looking down. "The goblins pulled him in with them."

Curtis squatted down and looked at the seal. "It looks like the seal is still open, though," he said, frowning. "That means —"

Curtis stopped as the crack suddenly grew brighter and wider. Flo held up a hand to shield her eyes against the bright blue glare. As she watched in shock, a hair-covered paw emerged. A second later, another paw stuck out. The paws clawed the tile floor, trying to get a good grip.

"Help!" Furry's voice called from inside the crack. "Pull me up!"

Flo's heart raced. She grabbed Furry's right paw while Curtis grabbed the left. With a tug, they pulled Furry out of his world and back into theirs. As his feet passed back through the crack, the light dimmed and the gap seemed to shrink.

The three of them collapsed on the dingy laundry room floor.

"You're back," Flo whispered. She sat up,

a giant smile on her face. "Back where you belong."

Furry was so out of breath he was panting, but he still managed to grin back at her. "I'm so happy I could howl right now," he said.

"Don't," Curtis said. "Last time you did that, some of the tenants heard. They were terrified. I had to make up a story about old pipes making that noise."

"How did you get back?" Flo asked. "I thought once you went through you were trapped there. That's what Snottle said. 'There's no coming back.'"

Flo leaned over and looked at the crack again. It was thinner and dimmer now, but it still glowed a steady, faint blue. It looked much brighter than it had when Furry had been inside.

"I'm not really sure," Furry said. "Snottle lost his grip, and I managed to dive back through before the seal closed."

"We need to cover this up before anything else comes through," Curtis said, standing up. "There's a good chance more monsters caught a whiff of you when you were in there. They'll be coming after you."

Curtis walked out of the room and returned with a large piece of plywood. "We use these to board up broken windows until the glass can be replaced," he explained. "Should do the trick here too."

He set the wood over the crack in the floor. "There," he said. "It's not a perfect fix, but it'll hold for the time being." He turned and gave Furry a pointed look. "That is, if you stop messing with it."

"I will," Furry said. He held a paw up to show he meant it. "Wolf's honor."

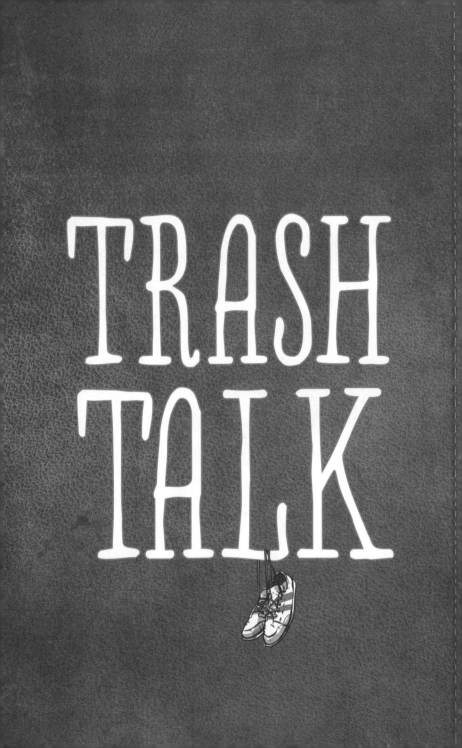

CHAPTER 11

After they'd covered the crack up again,
Curtis collected his clean laundry and turned
to head back to his apartment.

"You two had better clean up the mess the
goblins made. I don't do that anymore," he
said as he left the laundry room. "I'm retired."

"I know, I know," Furry said, rolling his eyes.
"We'll clean it up. Don't worry about it."

"So Curtis has known you're a werewolf

this whole time?" Flo whispered as she and Furry headed back to the trash room.

"He's the one who found me when I first came through," Furry said. "Hey, do you have anything else to drink in your lunchbox?"

"You're in luck," Flo said, opening her lunchbox and grabbing a juice box. "One left."

The werewolf gulped down the last of the juice in seconds flat. Then Furry let out a loud belch and transformed back into the human version of himself.

In moments, he looked like a normal boy again. If Flo didn't know any better, she would have thought nothing had happened. Only Furry's shredded shorts were out of the ordinary.

"Jeez, those shorts have seen better days," Flo said, pointing to Furry's destroyed pants.

"I'm in so much trouble," Furry said, shaking his head. "You have no idea how many pairs of pants I've ruined. My mom is going to kill me."

"Which mom?" Flo asked. "Those goblins made it sound like the Babbitts aren't your real parents. But I met your mom last week."

Furry avoided her gaze. "Well . . ." he started to say.

"You'd better start from the begining," Flo said. "You said Curtis found you when you came through the crack in the floor, right?"

Furry nodded. "He was fixing a dryer," he explained. "He said the floor rumbled behind him and split open all of a sudden. He thought it was an earthquake or something."

"I'll bet," Flo said.

"But instead, I came through," Furry

explained. "I was just a puppy then. Curtis gave me something to eat and drink at his apartment. It wasn't until I burped and turned into a human for the first time that Curtis realized what I was."

"Wow," Flo said. "So how did you end up with the Babbitts? Does that mean they know you're a . . . ?"

Furry shook his head. "No. Curtis is friends with Mona's husband, Jorge," he explained. "He knew they always wanted a kid, so he asked them to watch after me. I had to promise him I wouldn't change in front of them. That's why I go up to the roof or hide in the basement when there's a full moon."

Flo's jaw dropped. "So not even your parents know you're a werewolf?" she asked in disbelief.

"Nope," Furry said. "Not so far, anyway. You and Curtis are the only ones who know."

Flo was amazed. She couldn't hide anything from her mom. She'd tried to sneak a stray cat into their house once, and her mom had found out almost immediately. But for Furry to hide what he truly was? He had to be good at lying.

No wonder I didn't realize where he's really from, Flo thought.

When they reached the trash room, Furry and Flo groaned. The goblins had shredded most of the trash bags and flung garbage everywhere. Shattered glass littered the floor. There was even garbage smeared on the walls.

"It's going to take forever to clean this up," Flo complained. She plugged her nose against the smell. "Ugh! This is so disgusting!"

"Now I'm wishing I would've gone with the goblins," Furry said. "Then I wouldn't have to clean." When he saw Flo glaring at him, he grinned. "Kidding."

* * *

Furry and Flo worked for more than an hour before they took a break. When they couldn't stand the smell anymore, they stepped into the hallway and sat down with their backs against the wall.

Flo brushed her hands off and opened her lunchbox. She pulled out a sandwich, already cut down the middle, and tossed one half to Furry. He devoured the whole thing down in two bites and looked over at her half of the sandwich hungrily. Flo sighed and tossed him her half. He inhaled it just as quickly and wiped his mouth.

"Why were those goblins so determined to bring you back with them?" Flo asked when Furry had finished eating. "Why can't they just leave you here? What do they care?"

"Because I broke the seal when I came through," Furry explained. "They want it closed again. They're afraid of what could happen if anyone else from here finds out about it."

A world of monsters afraid of humans coming into their world? she thought. *How do they think we feel?*

"So as long as it's open, more giant spiders, goblins, and who knows what else can get through?" Flo said.

Furry nodded, but he avoided her gaze. "As long as I'm here, the seal stays open."

"But Curtis blocked it off," Flo said. "Right?"

"Sort of," Furry said. "For now."

Flo looked down at her open lunchbox. She knew it was selfish and dangerous, but she was glad her world had Furry in it. For the time being, it didn't matter that their apartment building, the city, and the rest of the world might end up in danger.

For now her friend was back, and that was all that mattered.

THE AUTHOR

Thomas Kingsley Troupe writes, makes movies, and works as a firefighter/EMT. He's written many books for kids, including *Legend of the Vampire* and *Mountain Bike Hero*, and has two boys of his own. He likes zombies, bacon, orange Popsicles, and reading stories to his kids. Thomas currently lives in Woodbury, Minnesota, with his super cool family.

THE ILLUSTRATOR

Stephen Gilpin is the illustrator of several dozen children's books and is currently working on a project he hopes will give him the ability to walk through walls — although he acknowledges there is still a lot of work to be done on this project. He currently lives in Hiawatha, Kansas, with his genius wife, Angie, and their kids.

THE MISPLACED MUMMY

As Flo stared at the horizon, something howled and landed behind her with a loud *THUMP!*

Flo turned around to see Furry, in his werewolf form, lying on his back in the hot sand. The little werewolf leapt up onto his paws and shook the sand from his fur.

"Dang, this sand gets everywhere," Furry muttered. His tongue hung out of his mouth, and he panted in the scorching heat. "And it's hot here."

"Where is here exactly?" Flo aske looking around.

"My world," Furry said. "My old one, I mean. And coming here was not one of your better ideas."

Flo looked back toward the desert city and the enormous pyramids. "No one asked you to follow me," she said.

"Well I couldn't just leave you here all alone," Furry said. "Besides, my shard is in your lunchbox, remember? I have to get it back."

Furry turned and started digging in the sand. In moments, he'd uncovered a small stone circle embedded in the sand. It looked like a platform of some kind. The edges were worn, but a decorative pattern ran around the outside.

"This is our way back," Furry said. "But only until the sun sets."

Flo crossed her arms. "What happens at sunset?" she asks.

"We're stuck here forever," Furry whispered.

WANT MORE ADVENTURE?

FIND IT AT
WWW.CAPSTONEKIDS.COM